Grow

JoAnn Early Macken

Illustrated by
Stephanie Fizer Coleman

BOYDS MILLS PRESS

AN IMPRINT OF BOYDS MILLS & KANE

New York

Boyds Mills Press
An imprint of Boyds Mills & Kane, a division of Astra Publishing House
boydsmillspress.com
Printed in China

ISBN: 978-1-63592-308-7 (hc)
ISBN: 978-1-63592-376-6 (eBook)
Library of Congress Control Number: 2020931563

First edition
10 9 8 7 6 5 4 3 2 1

Design by Barbara Grzeslo
The text is set in Neutraface Demi.
The illustrations are done digitally and
include hand-painted textures.

For Gene,
growing ever dearer
—JEM

For Seth, always
—SFC

If you were an acorn, you'd swing from a stout twig, snug inside a hard brown shell, bristled cap on your head.

One day, you'd drop to the leafy floor. Slowly, you'd crack your jacket. Then bit by bit, year after year, you'd stretch roots into soil and trunk and limbs into sky.

You'd be an oak tree, reaching lobed
leaves toward sunlight.

If you were a caterpillar, you'd
inch over milkweed, munching,
stripes blending in with shadows
and stems, shedding your skin
when it grew too tight.

You'd button yourself to a leaf, molt one last time, and wriggle into a blue-green chrysalis. After a while, you'd pop out, unfold orange wings, and flutter from flower to flower.

You'd be a monarch butterfly, sipping sweet nectar from windblown blooms.

If you were a tadpole, you'd swish and dart in a mossy pond, breathe murky water through gills and slick skin, nibble on green waterweeds.

Gradually, you'd grow legs, back and front.
They'd lengthen and strengthen. Your tail
would shrink. One day, breathing air into
lungs, you'd crawl onto land, hop after prey,
and snatch it with your long, sticky tongue.

You'd be a leopard frog, leaping through rustling reeds.

If you were a hatchling, you'd climb up
through soft, sandy soil, scurry past
long-legged wading birds, and burrow
into a muddy streambed.

Your shell would protect your head, legs, and tail, growing larger each year, shedding old scutes as new ones formed underneath. On warm days, you'd bask on a sunlit log.

You'd be a painted turtle, plopping into
a rippling pond.

If you were a duckling, you'd waddle to water, following your mother and sisters and brothers—all downy fluff, flapping and peeping and pecking.

Over the summer, you'd trade
down for feathers. You'd forage in
foliage, dabble upended, learn how to fly,
and flap to the sky! Come fall, you'd join
a flock winging south.

You'd be a mallard duck, migrating over cities and farms.

If you were a fawn, you'd rest among ferns and soft grasses, hidden in dappled sunlight, speckled and shy, waiting.

You'd stand on spindly legs. First, you'd wobble. Later, lankier, you'd sprint and then spring. You'd wander on trails through forest and field, leaving heart-shaped tracks as you browsed.

You'd be a white-tailed deer, bounding along roadsides and riverbanks.

When you were a baby, snug in a blanket,
you gazed at the world, bright eyes open
wide, holding onto a finger with your
whole tiny hand. You babbled and cooed.
You listened and learned.

Now look at you! Look at all you can do: splash in the shallows like turtles and ducks, search for an acorn, a tadpole, a butterfly, leave your dear footprints wherever you go.

You're the only true you, unlike any
other in this whole dazzling world.
You're finding your own way to . . .

. . . grow.